# PUPPY & BEAR

## The First Day of School

written by Larry Dane Brimner

illustrated by John Bendall-Brunello

two lions

To Children Everywhere, who have ever been
loved by a pet, with thanks to Joan Sandin.
—L.D.B.

To my wonderful wife, Tiziana, and of course,
to Millie, our sweet little dog.
—J.B-B.

Published by Two Lions, New York
www.apub.com
Amazon, the Amazon logo, and Two Lions are trademarks of
Amazon.com, Inc., or its affiliates.

ISBN-13: 9781503950962 (hardcover)
ISBN-10: 1503950964 (hardcover)

The illustrations are rendered in
watercolor and colored pencil.
Book design by Vera Soki

Printed in China

First Edition
10 9 8 7 6 5 4 3 2 1

**Puppy found Bear**
sitting alone against an old,
gnarled oak tree and got
so excited, he ran in circles.
Maybe we could be friends,
he thought.

Puppy bounced over. "Who are you?"

"It's none of your beeswax, but I'm Bear," said Bear. "I'm a bear who is bored. There's nothing to do."

"We could play," said Puppy, showing Bear his favorite ball.

Bear rolled his eyes. "You're just a puppy. You probably can't even catch a ball."

"Well, I'm the best chaser in the world," Puppy said.

He tossed the ball to show Bear . . .

. . . but Bear reached out with one paw and caught it.
"Maybe I can teach you how to catch," he said.

After that the two played catch-the-ball and chase and hide-and-seek beneath the oak trees . . . until Bear forgot all about being bored.

That Summer, Bear helped Puppy climb up in the basket of his bicycle and they sailed down the dirt lane past the empty schoolhouse.

Bear liked to pedal fast.
Puppy liked the way his long ears flapped like a
bird's wings in the breeze.

Sometimes they pretended the giant boulder was a pirate ship, the *S. S. Rex*, and they were its captain and crew. Puppy liked when the captain growled,

"walk the plank, Matey!"

Bear was a good growler, and no one jumped better than Puppy.

When it got really hot, they waded in the creek, laughing at their rippled reflections.

"You look like Big Foot," said Puppy.

Bear snorted. "Well, you look like Big Toe, and I'm going to splash you!"

"I'll splash you first!!!" shouted Puppy.

Soon they were both dripping.

All summer, they met every morning at the old, gnarled oak tree to romp and roam and run . . . until the sun grew weary and tucked itself in at night.

But one morning, Bear didn't come to the tree.
Puppy waited and waited. He wandered through
the fields where they played and looked out from
the deck of the *S. S. Rex*.

He waded in the creek, but his was
the only rippled reflection in the water.
"Maybe Bear got lost," he said.

Puppy searched and searched until
finally he saw Bear skipping down the
lane! He bounced up beside Bear and
dropped his ball. "Let's play," he said.

"Today is the first day of school,"
said Bear. "I don't want to be late."

Puppy tried again. This time he batted
the ball with his paw.

"I better hurry,"
said Bear, and he rushed on.

Puppy watched . . .

as Bear dashed into the schoolhouse.
Why was Bear in such a hurry?

He watched at lunchtime . . . as Bear laughed and played games on the playground. Puppy felt sad now, remembering the fun he and Bear had had all summer long.

He watched at the end of the day . . . as Bear
bounded out the schoolhouse door. But Bear was so
fast he was gone before Puppy could find his ball.
Didn't Bear want to be his friend anymore?
Puppy slumped away.

Puppy tossed his ball this way and that.
But he couldn't throw it as far as Bear.

He played hide-and-seek by himself.
But Bear knew all the best hiding places.

"Walk the plank!" he shouted, trying to growl like Bear, and he jumped. But what fun was that without his captain?

Finally, Puppy curled up beneath the old, gnarled oak tree.

"What's wrong, Puppy?" asked Bear.
"You didn't play with me today,"
said Puppy.
"That's because I am old enough
for school now. But I ran all the
way home so we could play together
before it gets dark."

"Really?" asked Puppy.
"Really," said Bear, and he gave
Puppy a big bear hug. "We go together
like bread and honey.

We're best friends,
you and me."

Bear picked up Puppy's ball and tossed it.
From then on, Puppy and Bear met at their
tree every day after school.
They raced through the autumn leaves.

They took turns walking the plank and splashing into winter's snowy sea.

They went on long, long bicycle rides, with Puppy's ears flapping in the spring breeze.
Soon it would be summer again. And then fall.
And then Puppy would go to school, too.

Puppy and Bear were best friends, in and out of days, and in and out of seasons.

Forever.